MW01251084

DEMCO

★ *GREAT SPORTS TEAMS* ★

THE SAN ANTONIO

BASKETBALL TEAM

Glenn Rogers

Enslow Publishers, Inc.
44 Fadem Road   PO Box 38
Box 699   Aldershot
Springfield, NJ 07081   Hants GU12 6BP
USA   UK

Library of Congress Cataloging-in-Publication Data

Rogers, Glenn.
    The San Antonio Spurs basketball team / Glenn Rogers.
        p. cm. — (Great sports teams)
    Includes bibliographical references (p.) and index.
    Summary: Traces the history of the Texas team that has featured such stars
as George Gervin and David Robinson, discussing key personalities and
games over the past twenty-three years.
    ISBN 0-89490-797-2
    1. San Antonio Spurs (Basketball team)—Juvenile literature. [1. San Antonio
Spurs (Basketball team)—History. 2. Basketball—History.] I. Title. II. Series.
GV885.52.S26R65 1997
796.323′64′09764351—dc20   96-46527
                                                       CIP
                                                       AC

CONTENTS

*J*ohnny Moore was a member of the San
Antonio Spurs during the 1981–82 season.
That season the Spurs and the Bucks played one
of the most memorable NBA games.

BIG NUMBERS

San Antonio's twenty-three-year history has been packed with thrilling moments. There have been countless last-second wins and losses, and games settled by buzzer-beating dunks. There have been three-point bombs, and nerve-wracking misses followed by instant, game-saving put-backs.

The Spurs have engaged in ferocious playoffs, including epic struggles with the Los Angeles Lakers in two Western Conference Finals. These matches pitted superstar George Gervin against Kareem Abdul-Jabbar and Magic Johnson. David Robinson guided his Spurs to a rousing six-game battle against the Houston Rockets in the 1994 Western Conference Finals.

Perhaps the most exhilarating single-game happening came on March 6, 1982. More than 11,700 fans witnessed a memorable triple-overtime struggle against the invading Milwaukee Bucks at the

Hemis-Fair Arena. The roller-coaster ride left the fans gasping, cheering, and groaning. The Spurs took, lost, and again took leads.

It was nip and tuck from the beginning, but the Spurs looked as if they had the game in the bag. They led by three, with just nine seconds left in regulation time. Then Milwaukee's Brian Winters, who scored 42 points, hit a three-pointer at the buzzer to tie the contest and send it into the first overtime. Winters hit the shot, despite Spurs guard Johnny Moore's standing practically in his face just beyond the three-point line.

"I couldn't believe it," said Moore. "He just let it fly."[1] Matters appeared grim for the San Antonio fans when the Bucks took a 143–141 lead, with seconds left in the first overtime. The Bucks' defenders refused to allow an open shot, and Dave Corzine made a desperation heave from the corner. His try bounced off the rim, but Mike Mitchell tipped the ball back in to tie, the second the clock ran out.

Milwaukee again appeared ready to send the Arena fans home unhappy when they led by two with just twenty-six seconds left to play. Again, Corzine entered the picture. The Spurs' big center scored on a layup to tie the game, 155–155.

Finally, the Spurs took control in the third overtime. Scoring machine Gervin connected with a five-foot hook shot ninety seconds into the last overtime to put San Antonio ahead, 159–157, and the Spurs never trailed again.

His shot came just after Winters had tied the game by hitting his thirteenth straight shot. That was it,

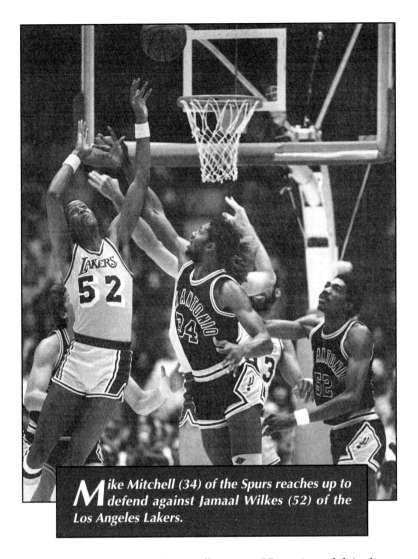

Mike Mitchell (34) of the Spurs reaches up to defend against Jamaal Wilkes (52) of the Los Angeles Lakers.

though, for the Bucks' rifleman. He missed his last three tries.

"We knew that Brian would miss sooner or later," Gervin said. He finally did after lucky No. 13 (Winters had hit 13 straight shots).[2]

The Spurs puffed up to a 167–161 lead—incredibly enough, matching the largest spread between the two

George Gervin extends himself to avoid the hand of the New Orleans Jazz's Joe Meriweather.

teams throughout the long contest—and then held off the Bucks by hitting their free throws. Finally, the Spurs emerged with a 171–166 victory. The 171 points are the fourth highest single-game total in NBA history, and the combined 337 points are the second highest.

"This was the best shooting game I've ever seen," said then Spurs' coach Stanley Albeck, referring to the incredible 61.2 percent firing by Milwaukee and the answering 58.6 percent barrage from San Antonio.[3]

"This was a game these guys will cherish for the rest of their lives," said Albeck. "This is what pro basketball is supposed to be about."[4]

Gervin, the Iceman of the NBA, had 50 points in the game, including 24 during the overtimes and 8 straight hits. "It was the most exciting game I've ever played in," Gervin still says.[5]

There were plenty of heroes escorting Gervin and Winters. Mitchell, of course, with his vital tip-in, also scored 45 points. Moore handed out 16 assists.

Milwaukee's Junior Bridgeman and Bob Lanier helped keep the Arena fans on the edge of their seats by scoring 31 and 29 points, respectively, and bothering the Spurs all night with their sporadic and irritating defense.

The San Antonio Spurs were first known as the Texas, and later Dallas, Chaparrals of the American Basketball Association (ABA). Dallas is shown here in a game against the Utah Stars.

THE BEGINNING

The Dallas Chaparrals were an ABA team working in front of minuscule audiences. The team was on the brink of bankruptcy. The owners were looking for financial relief, a way out.

Their problems were observed by San Antonio businessman Jack Pitluk. He contacted entrepreneurs Red McCombs and Angelo Drossos. Drossos, a stockbrocker, took charge of the situation.

Drossos gathered about twenty other investors, including McCombs. They arranged to borrow the Chaps, taking the team to San Antonio on a lend-lease deal. This was the deal: The San Antonians would pay $800,000 with the option to buy outright for $4.6 million within two years.

Renamed the Spurs, the team played its first game in 1973. The team was greeted by a relatively small but boisterous and loud crowd of about four thousand people. The crowd was ignited by a core group of fanatics known as the Baseline Bums.

Drossos, elected by the various investors to run the team, figured he had a winner on his hands, and he persuaded his fellow investors to purchase the Dallas team outright within the first six months. "A lot of the guys did it for the write-off, some did it because they thought basketball would be good for the city," Drossos said of that time. "Nobody figured they would make any money."[1]

Drossos managed with a fine eye on the bottom line, though. The team lost money during only one year of his tenure, which lasted until McCombs bought him out during the summer of 1988. Drossos sold players for cash, and bargained hard with them during contract negotiations. He kept base salaries low by installing an innovative contract clause that paid incentive money for wins over thirty-five games.

Drossos juiced up his team during the first year. He brought in ABA stars Swen Nater and George Gervin, and kept Dallas star James Silas. The team was an almost immediate success, winning 51 games during the 1974–75 campaign. Still, the Spurs almost drifted into the history books when the NBA made its powerful move to eliminate the ABA and the competition for basketball fans.

The sparkling talents of Gervin, Julius Erving, David Thompson, Connie Hawkins, and Spencer Haywood were nabbing headlines and drawing rabid fans, eating into the NBA domain. Nevertheless, the ABA was tottering on the brink of financial ruin. The NBA was on more solid ground, but still eons away from the glory days of Larry Bird and Magic Johnson.

The San Antonio Spurs Basketball Team

*A*llan Bristow of the San Antonio Spurs has all he can handle in trying to guard Julius Erving, one of the greatest stars of the ABA.

In 1976, four ABA teams were merged into the NBA. Angelo Drossos is pictured here with ABA Commissioner Dave DeBusschere (center) and New York Nets owner Roy Boe.

The two leagues had discussed merging, but matters didn't come to a head until the summer of 1976, when the ABA threatened to launch an antitrust suit against the NBA. The two leagues met in Hyannis Port, Massachusetts, to thrash out the problems.

"I thought that we didn't have a deal, the NBA kept asking for too much money," Drossos recalls. "I told the other ABA owners that we would just have to go back home and fight the other league in the courts."[2]

Then, on the evening of the last day of talks, Drossos was summoned from his room. "I was already packed and ready to go home," he said. "I got a call and went to the NBA's meeting room in my slippers. They just said, 'Angelo, we've got a deal.'"[3]

The net result: Four teams from the ABA—San Antonio, Denver, New York (now the New Jersey Nets), and Indiana—were allowed into the NBA for $3 million each. The rest of the ABA players were dispersed in a general draft.

*U*sing his strength, David Robinson looks to get off the shot. When Robinson arrived for the 1989–90 season the Spurs went from a last place team to a playoff contender.

OUTSTANDING SPURS

A parade of great players has marched in San Antonio. George Gervin and David Robinson lead this procession of outstanding talents who have brought national and international attention to the Spurs in central Texas.

George Gervin

Gervin's airy feats with the round ball—first the red, white, and blue in the ABA, then the solid brown of the NBA—rivaled those of yet-to-come megastar Michael Jordan and placed San Antonio firmly on the map of professional hoops.

Gervin, known as the Iceman in the basketball world and GG to his friends, played twelve years with the Spurs. He led the NBA in scoring four times (three consecutive years), played in nine NBA All-Star Games, and was recently inducted into the Naismith Memorial Basketball Hall of Fame in Springfield, Massachusetts.

George Gervin, (center), known to basketball fans as The Iceman, celebrates with David Thompson and Gail Goodrich prior to their Hall of Fame induction ceremony.

"Ice had more polish, a better variety of shots and more ways to score than Julius Erving," says former Spurs coach Doug Moe. In short, Gervin was unstoppable.[1]

During his three years in the ABA, Gervin averaged 22.2 points. His scoring agility increased when Coach Bob Bass switched him from forward to guard, and he averaged 27.3 points during his nine years with the NBA Spurs. "I'd like to say that was a stroke of genius, but, the truth is, James Silas was hurt and we needed to change the guard situation," Bass says.[2]

Gervin astounded Arena crowds when he resembled a pinball, bouncing off defenders while he was in

The San Antonio Spurs Basketball Team

the air, and drifting toward the bucket. He won his first scoring title when he astonished the crowd in New Orleans by scoring 63 points in the last game of the 1977–78 season. He had needed fifty-eight points to nose out the Nuggets' David Thompson.

David Robinson

David Robinson, the Admiral, never played with Gervin, but he saved the franchise when he arrived for the 1989–90 season after completing two years in the Navy. He was a phenomenal player at the Naval Academy and the first player chosen in the 1987 draft.

Robinson towered at seven feet one inch, but he had the agility, coordination, and running ability of the swiftest guards. He easily won all the sprint races during the team's practice session, often finishing the dashes laughing and running backward.

Robinson electrified crowds with his high-bounding dunks and his slashing moves through defenders. He generated as much excitement with his leaping blocks, at times smashing back power dunk attempts.

The Spurs' center has won almost every major award. He was Most Valuable Player of the 1994–95 season, Defensive Player of the Year in 1992, and top rookie in 1990. He has been the league's top rebounder, top shot blocker, and top scorer.

He won the scoring title when he edged out Shaquille O'Neal by scoring 71 points against the Clippers on the last day of the 1993–94 campaign.

Robinson is an NBA oddity. The usual pro star's background includes a few playground raves, eighth-grade heroics, high school spotlights, and college recruiting wars, but Robinson had none of this. He played a bit of junior high ball, but then he quit. He played during his senior year in high school "because it was fun." Thinking no more of it, he entered the Naval Academy, hoping to become an engineer. His problem "was that growing up, he didn't know if he wanted to be Mozart, Thomas Edison, or Bon Jovi," former Spurs coach Larry Brown said.[3]

James Silas

James Silas never received the generous national fame showered on Gervin and Robinson, but he was the spark that ignited the early ABA and NBA Spurs.

He was dubbed Captain Late because of his propensity for hitting last-second game-winning baskets. It was Silas, not Gervin, who usually got the ball after the last time-out in those down-the-stretch games.

Silas played three years for the Spurs in the ABA and averaged 19.6 points. He suffered a serious knee injury, struggled for two years, but then averaged 17.7 points during his last two years with San Antonio, 1979–81.

Many fans think the Spurs could have gone on to win the 1976 ABA title, if Silas hadn't broken his ankle in Game 1 of the series against the New York Nets. The Spurs lost the series, 4–3.

James Silas faces the basket to get off a shot against the Philadelphia 76ers. Silas was known as Captain Late because of his ability to hit last second shots with the game on the line.

*B*ob Bass has served as both head coach and general manager of the San Antonio Spurs. Bass was responsible for many personnel moves, including the signing of David Robinson.

GREAT LEADERS

The coaches who have suffered and rejoiced along the sidelines have included Tom Nissalke, Bob Bass, Doug Moe, Stan Albeck, Cotton Fitzsimmons, John Lucas, and now Greg Popovich. Even University of Nevada, Las Vegas, legend Jerry Tarkanian coached the Spurs for twenty games. Here are some of the many coaches and behind-the-scenes men who have made a difference.

Bob Bass

Bass surely enjoyed the most unusual run as coach. He first took over the reins when Tom Nissalke was fired midway through the 1974–75 season. He held control until he went back to the front office after the 1975–76 season, having won 50 games that season and losing to the New York Nets in seven games in the opening round of the playoffs.

Bass also served as assistant coach under Doug Moe for three and a half seasons, becoming head coach again when Moe was fired in March 1980. Bass did two more stints as head coach, replacing the fired Mo McHone during the 1983–84 campaign and the fired Larry Brown during the 1991–92 year.

"I always said I'd never again coach a team that I hadn't been with during training camp, but I kept doing it," Bass said.[1]

Bass served as general manager and then vice president of basketball operations for most of his tenure in San Antonio, overseeing the bulk of the major moves, including trading George Gervin, signing David Robinson, drafting Sean Elliott, Willie Anderson, and Alvin Robertson, and trading for Artis Gilmore, Mike Mitchell, and Dennis Rodman.

Larry Brown

Larry Brown, known as the nomad of professional basketball, came to the Spurs in 1988, fresh on the heels of winning the NCAA title with Kansas. The charismatic Brown lit the fires of optimism in San Antonio. During the summer prior to his first year, he attracted crowds of hundreds during appearances at local shopping malls.

Brown came hoping that the Navy would release David Robinson from his final year of active service obligation. The hopes were dashed, and Brown suffered through the franchise's worst season. They finished in second to last place in their division, 21-61.

*L*arry Brown came aboard to coach the Spurs in 1988. The following year, he and David Robinson led the Spurs to first place in the Midwest Division.

Then, when Robinson arrived for the 1989–90 season, Brown's prospects changed dramatically. Brown and the Admiral led the Spurs to a 52-26 record and a monumental battle against the experienced Portland Trail Blazers in the Western Conference Semifinals. San Antonio fell in overtime in game seven at Portland.

Cotton Fitzsimmons

Cotton Fitzsimmons coached two years (1984–86) in San Antonio. He caught the Spurs on the downslide. Fitzsimmons took the heavy blame for trading George Gervin. The raspy-voiced veteran coach seldom complained but the fans were murderous. They booed every announcement of his name at games. Fitzsimmons later coached the Phoenix Suns.

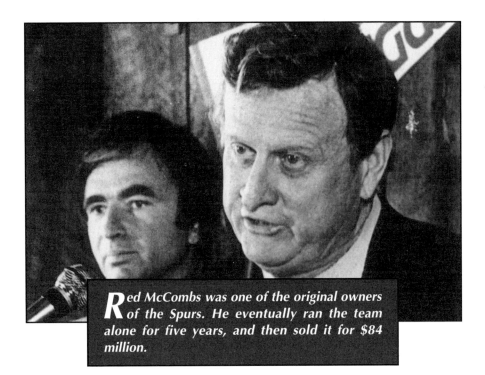

*R*ed McCombs was one of the original owners of the Spurs. He eventually ran the team alone for five years, and then sold it for $84 million.

Angelo Drossos

Angelo Drossos was a stockbrocker and sports enthusiast. Prior to becoming the major management figure in the Spurs' early life, he promoted boxing events throughout Texas.

Drossos was a bottom-line man. He watched the pennies and traded players for cash. He once battled Coach Stan Albeck through the courts when Albeck quit the Spurs to coach the New Jersey Nets. Drossos received money and a player (Fred Roberts) in return for Albeck's leaving.

Operating in the league's smallest market, Drossos's team earned money in all but one of his fourteen years at the helm. Drossos is called the

The San Antonio Spurs Basketball Team

Father of the Salary Cap. It was his idea for the NBA to put a lid on teams' salaries. The cap would keep the smaller-market teams competitive against the teams in larger metropolitan areas. San Antonio has a population of about 1.5 million, compared with New York's nearly 20 million.

Drossos continued operating the team until he sold his interest to McCombs. Drossos received $17 million from McCombs, a massive increase over his original investment of about $10,000. Drossos's last major act was the signing of David Robinson.

Red McCombs

Red McCombs provided most of the financial muscle for the initial band of investors to purchase the Spurs. He remained behind the scenes, even took a three-year sabbatical when he owned the Denver Nuggets, but always provided the local news outlets with colorful quotes regarding the team's status.

McCombs, owner of automobile dealerships throughout Texas and Colorado, was a flash-and-dash man. He bellowed and barked. He brought in the colorful Larry Brown to coach, raised ticket prices, talked about championships, and awaited the arrival of the franchise savior, David Robinson.

McCombs ran the ship alone for just five years. He sold the team to a group of local businessmen for $84 million in 1993.

*G*eorge Gervin looks to drive to the basket against Elvin Hayes of the Washington Bullets. The Spurs faced the Bullets in the 1979 Eastern Conference Finals.

SHINING SEASONS

The Spurs took root in San Antonio during the heyday of the ABA. The team flourished, and it remains at the top of the game. The franchise has missed the playoffs only three times during its twenty-three-year history, and has contested in the NBA Conference Finals four times, coming closest to the finals when it fell, 4–3, to the Washington Bullets in 1979.

The franchise could floor a powerhouse team if players from different eras could suddenly become teammates. One mighty entry could be David Robinson at center, Terry Cummings at power forward, Chuck Person at small forward, George Gervin at shooting guard, and James Silas at the point. Backing up these stalwarts could be Artis Gilmore, Dennis Rodman, Mike Mitchell, Alvin Robertson, and Johnny Moore.

The perennial question around San Antonio is: Which team boasted the greatest lineup?

1978-79

Some say the team that took on the Bullets in 1979 was certainly not the best San Antonio entry, but maybe the scrappiest.

That squad looked ready to march right into the finals when it took a 3–1 lead on the Bullets in that Eastern Conference Finals series. That was when Bullets coach Dick Motta made his infamous pronouncement: "It ain't over until the Fat Lady sings."[1] Indeed. Alamo City hearts were broken when the Bullets won the next three games. The end came when forward Bobby Dandridge hit a jumper with eight seconds left, to give Washington a 107–105 win in game seven.

The Spurs' starting lineup was Mark Olberding, Larry Kenon, Mike Green, George Gervin, and James Silas.

The 1980s

The Spurs had problems getting by the Los Angeles Lakers in the early 1980s, but they still battled the then world champions in the Western Conference Finals in 1983.

The Spurs fell, four games to two, losing the fourth when Magic Johnson blocked a Mike Mitchell shot in the final seconds.

That team looked considerably stronger than the 1979 entry. It boasted Artis Gilmore at center, surrounded

*A*rtis Gilmore, Edgar Jones, George Gervin, and Mike Dunleavy (left to right) look on during a 1983 playoff loss to the Lakers.

by George Gervin, Mike Mitchell, Gene Banks, and Johnny Moore as starters. During the 1982–83 season, Gervin averaged 26.2 points, Mitchell 19.9, Gilmore 18, Banks 14.9, and Moore 12.2.

Gervin and Gilmore were All-Stars that year, and Gervin was named to the All-NBA team.

"That was surely one of our greatest teams," says Bob Bass. "We had the misfortune of running into that great Laker team that had Kareem Abdul-Jabbar, Magic Johnson, and James Worthy."[2]

Shining Seasons

Gliding through the air, Sean Elliot attempts to shoot over Carl Herrera of the Houston Rockets, as David Robinson positions himself for a possible pass.

The Spurs had their ups and downs through the next several years. They were rejuvenated when David Robinson, Sean Elliott, and Terry Cummings all joined the team at the start of the 1989–90 season.

Now fans who were engrossed in coming up with the greatest Spurs lineup start talking about that club, which advanced to the Western Conference Semifinals and battled the eventual Western Conference Champion Portland Trail Blazers. The Spurs easily defeated the Blazers at the Arena in San Antonio but lost three close games in Portland, the final one, Game 7, in overtime.

Rounding out that team's starters, alongside Robinson, Elliott, and Cummings, were Rod Strickland and Willie Anderson.

The Spurs, anchored by Robinson, then enjoyed strong regular seasons but sputtered in the playoffs until the 1994–95 campaign.

San Antonio won a franchise record and league high 62 regular season games. They pushed the eventual world champion Houston Rockets in the Western Conference Finals before falling in six games.

That lineup had a starting crew of Robinson, Dennis Rodman, Sean Elliott, Vinny Del Negro, and Avery Johnson, with Chuck Person coming off the bench for scoring power. "I'm disappointed that we lost our home court advantage, put ourselves in the position of losing the series on their court," said Coach Bob Hill. "But I'm proud of our effort."[3]

*J*ust fooling around, Robert Horry of the Houston Rockets, gives the Spurs Avery Johnson a punch in the face. Johnson, the point guard, is responsible for leading the team's attacks.

ONWARD AND UPWARD

common complaint from Spurs players, particularly David Robinson, was the franchise's habit of trading players, allowing players to drift into free agency, changing the makeup of the team, as well as changing coaches. The players wanted to build through solidarity.

Executive vice president Gregg Popovich, brought in to run the show after the 1993–94 season, has vowed that a core group of players, the principal starters, will remain with the team through several years.

"It's the first time we've had that here," says Avery Johnson, the five-foot eleven-inch wonder who guides the team's attacks at the point guard position. "We have to remember that teams like Chicago, Detroit, the Lakers, most of the championship teams, always had the same main starters for several years."[1]

The team has a championship-contending look to it. Robinson is the foundation, and he's surrounded by a cast that includes Charles Smith, Chuck Person, Sean Elliott, Vinny Del Negro, and Will Perdue.

Robinson signed a new six-year contract worth $66 million at the start of the 1995–96 season. He has grown tremendously as a player. Early in his career, he had some troubles maintaining the essential single-minded concentration while on the floor, and with all his abilities, he lacked some of the basic footwork of the big man under the basket.

Now he says he wants a title. He has demonstrated that he has the charging energy needed to win games down the stretch. He has added a deft hook shot, a deadly jumper, and some slashing moves to his already overpowering game.

"The talent is here and it's a great bunch of guys," says Coach Bob Hill. "There's no doubt in my mind that we can win it all. We just have to take that next step of gutting it through some tough moments during the playoffs."[2]

The new group of owners backs Popovich to the hilt. There had been rumors through the years that outside owners would purchase the Spurs and move them to a more lucrative TV market, like Southern California or New Orleans. However, local businessmen, first spearheaded by Robert McDermott and then Peter Holt, have vowed to keep the team in the Alamo City.

San Antonio fans remain enthusiastic about their team and now just thirst for the ultimate thrill—the

The Spurs signed up superstar Dominique Wilkins in 1996.

NBA title. Visiting teams know about the noise and chants that can rain down on them when they take on the local heroes. In particular, opposing players are familiar with the Baseline Bums.

This core group of fanatical cheerers first formed when the Spurs arrived from Dallas in 1973. They purchased seats along the baseline (along courtside, at the ends of the court) during the early years in the Arena. The Bums group still exists, and some of them have had season tickets since the very beginning.

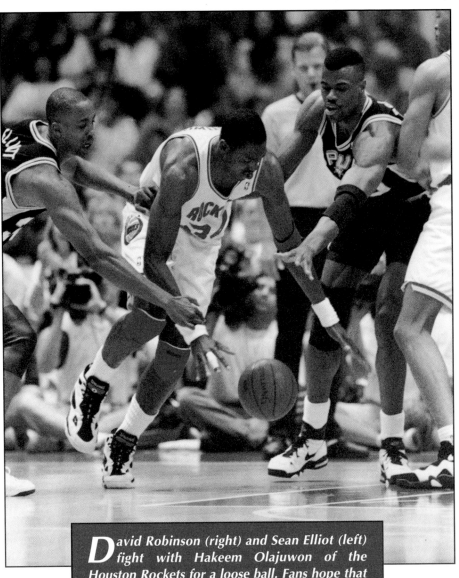

David Robinson (right) and Sean Elliot (left) fight with Hakeem Olajuwon of the Houston Rockets for a loose ball. Fans hope that Robinson can lead the team to its first NBA title.

The Spurs sit today almost at the edge of another era. The new owners are talking with city officials about the construction of a brand-new arena for the team. It will be a state-of-the-art building that will contain luxury suites, semiprivate seating, and a fine restaurant, and it will accommodate about twenty thousand fans.

The Spurs have rapped on the door to the NBA Finals four times, falling just short in the Conference Finals. "We've had a couple of real decent chances a couple of years since I've been here," Robinson says. "I really thought we would win it the year we had Dennis [Rodman] and again in 1996. But we've learned a lot; we still have the ability to win it all."[3] The Spurs hope to win an NBA championship just before they open their new playing court in the 1998–99 season.

STATISTICS

Team Record

SEASON	SEASON RECORD	PLAYOFF RECORD	COACH	DIVISION FINISH
1967–68	46-32	4-4	Cliff Hagan	2nd
1968–69	41-37	3-4	Cliff Hagan	4th
1969–70	45-39	2-4	Cliff Hagan, Max Williams	2nd
1970–71	30-54	1-4	Max Williams, Bill Blakely	4th
1971–72	42-42	0-4	Tom Nissalke	3rd
1972–73	28-56	—	Babe McCarthy Dave Brown	5th
1973–74	45-39	3-4	Tom Nissalke	3rd
1974–75	51-33	2-4	Tom Nissalke, Bob Bass	2nd
1975–76	50-34	3-4	Bob Bass	3rd
1976–77	44-38	0-2	Doug Moe	3rd
1977–78	52-30	2-4	Doug Moe	1st
1978–79	48-34	7-7	Doug Moe	1st
1979–80	41-41	1-2	Doug Moe Bob Bass	2nd
1980–81	52-30	3-4	Stan Albeck	1st
1981–82	48-34	4-5	Stan Albeck	1st
1982–83	53-29	6-5	Stan Albeck	1st
1983–84	37-45	—	Morris McHone, Bob Bass	5th
1984–85	41-41	2-3	Cotton Fitzsimmons	4th
1985–86	35-47	0-3	Cotton Fitzsimmons	6th
1986–87	28-54	—	Bob Weiss	6th
1987–88	21-61	—	Bob Weiss	5th
1988–89	31-51	0-3	Larry Brown	5th
1989–90	56-26	6-4	Larry Brown	1st

The San Antonio Spurs Basketball Team

Team Record (con't)

SEASON	SEASON RECORD	PLAYOFF RECORD	COACH	DIVISION FINISH
1990–91	55-27	1-3	Larry Brown	1st
1991–92	47-35	0-3	Larry Brown Bob Bass	2nd
1992–93	49-33	5-5	Jerry Tarkanian Rex Hughes, John Lucas	2nd
1993–94	55-27	3-4	John Lucas	2nd
1994–95	62-20	9-6	Bob Hill	1st
1995–96	59-23	5-5	Bob Hill	1st
1996–97	20-62	—	Bob Hill Gregg Popovich	6th
Totals	1,312-1,154	72-100		

Coaching Records

COACH	YEARS COACHED	RECORD	CHAMPIONSHIPS
Cliff Hagan	1967–70	109-90	None
Max Williams	1970–71	28-32	None
Bill Blakely	1970–71	25-40	None
Tom Nissalke	1971–72 1973–75	104-91	None
Babe McCarthy	1972–73	24-48	None
Dave Brown	1972–73	4-8	None
Bob Bass	1974–76 1979–80 1983–84 1991–92	144-108	None
Doug Moe	1976–80	177-135	Central Division 1977–78, 1978–79
Stan Albeck	1980–83	153-93	Midwest Division 1980–81, 1981–82,1982–83
Morris McHone	1983–84	11-20	None
Cotton Fitzsimmons	1984–86	76-88	None

Coaching Records (con't)

COACH	YEARS COACHED	RECORD	CHAMPIONSHIPS
Bob Weiss	1968–88	59-105	None
Larry Brown	1988–91	153-131	Midwest Division 1989–90, 1990–91
Jerry Tarkanian	1992	9-11	None
Rex Hughes	1992	1-0	None
John Lucas	1992–94	94-49	None
Bob Hill	1994–96	124-58	Midwest Division 1994–95, 1995–96
Gregg Popovich	1996–	17-47	None

Great Spurs

PLAYER	SEA	CAREER STATISTICS							
		YRS	G	REB	AST	BLK	STL	PTS	AVG
Terry Cummings	1989–95	15	1,037	7,985	2,064	622	1,158	18,355	17.7
Sean Elliot	1989–93 1994–	8	585	2,650	1,609	226	491	9,126	15.6
George Gervin	1973–85	14	1,060	5,602	2,798	—	—	26,595	25.1
Artis Gilmore	1982–87	17	1,329	16,330	3,050	—	—	24,941	18.8
Avery Johnson	1990–93 1994–97	9	630	1,107	3,697	90	682	5,432	8.6
Mike Mitchell	1981–88	10	759	4,246	1,010	400	530	15,016	19.8
Johnny Moore	1980–88 1989–90	9	520	1,548	3,866	116	1,017	4,890	9.4
Alvin Robertson	1984–89	12	779	4,428	3,773	323	2,132	10,882	14.0
David Robinson	1989–	8	563	6,614	1,726	2,012	940	14,366	25.5
James Silas	1972–81	10	685	2,069	2,628	—	—	11,038	16.1

SEA=Seasons with Spurs
YRS=Years in the NBA and ABA
G=Games

REB=Rebounds
AST=Assists
BLK=Blocks

STL=Steals
PTS=Total Points
AVG=Scoring Average

The San Antonio Spurs Basketball Team

CHAPTER NOTES

Chapter 1
1. Ray Evans, *San Antonio Light,* March 7, 1982, p. 4-F.
2. Mike Bruton, *San Antonio Express-News*, March 7, 1982, p. 8-S.
3. Ibid.
4. Evans, p. 4-F.
5. Conversation with the author.

Chapter 2
1. Glenn Rogers, *San Antonio Express-News*, April 11, 1993, p.10-C.
2. Ibid.
3. Ibid.

Chapter 3
1. Terry Pluto, *Loose Balls* (New York: Simon and Schuster, 1990), p. 311.
2. Ibid., p. 310.
3. Pat Jordan, "Kind David," *Sports Illustrated,* January 10, 1992, p. 172.

Chapter 4
1. Conversation with the author, during the latter half of the 1991–92 season.

Chapter 5
1. "It ain't over until the Fat Lady sings" is generally attributed to Dan Cook, television sportscaster and columnist for the *San Antonio Express-News.*
2. Conversation with the author.
3. Tom Orsborn, *San Antonio Express-News,* June 2, 1995, p. 1-S.

Chapter 6
1. Conversation with the author, after the trades that resulted in Houston's picking up Charles Barkley and the Lakers' signing Shaquille O'Neal.
2. Ibid.
3. Ibid.

GLOSSARY

ABA—The American Basketball Association. This group of teams was formed in 1967 and was brought together as an alternative to the National Basketball Association. It lasted nine seasons before merging with the NBA.

Alamodome—The Alamodome opened in the spring of 1993. It was built in hopes of attracting a National Football League team and has a seating capacity of over 65,000, including 60 luxury suites. The Spurs moved out of the Arena, and 1993–94 was their first season in the dome. One section of the structure was closed off for basketball, allowing a usual attendance capacity of over 21,000. For special games, the upper balconies are opened, and the capacity exceeds 35,000.

All-NBA Team—The five best players, usually named by position of center, two forwards, and two guards, named at the end of each NBA season.

bank shot—A ball that bounces off the backboard, the glass, before going into the net.

center—This is the Five Man, the team's tallest and, usually, strongest, player. The action of the guards and forwards revolves around the center, trying to get the ball into him for easy inside shots. Some centers, like David Robinson or Hakeem Olajuwon, also have solid jumpers from medium range. The center also has to be responsible for rebounding and defense.

dunk—This shot demands size, strength, and jumping ability. The player jumps, raises his arm over the rim, and just stuffs the ball through the net.

Hemis-Fair Arena—This was the original home of the Spurs when the team moved south from Dallas to San Antonio. It had a seating capacity of about 10,000. The roof was raised during the summer of 1977 to increase capacity by about 6,000.

hook shot—This shot usually is taken within eight feet, sometimes as far as fifteen feet, from the basket. The player stands sideways to the hoop and fires the ball to the basket with one hand over his head.

jump shot—The player jumps, usually to get space over a defender, brings the ball up into shooting position, and fires at the basket.

The San Antonio Spurs Basketball Team

layup—This shot comes from about three feet or closer from the basket. The player, usually after a drive or just playing under the basket, flips the ball up and into the net, sometimes banking it off the backboard.

NBA—The National Basketball Association. The group of professional basketball teams, like the Celtics or Spurs, that make up the league.

point guard—Often referred to as the One Guard. This is the team's lead guard, the player who directs the offense. He handles the ball most of the time, brings it up the court, and delivers it to the man in the best position to shoot it. Point guards include John Stockton and Anfernee Hardaway.

power forward—This is the Four Man. These players are the second biggest players on a team, after the center. They are counted on for rebounds, defense, and some inside scoring, usually layups or short jumpers. Everyone lists Karl Malone and Shawn Kemp as tops in this category.

put-back—A player grabs a teammate's missed shot under the basket and puts it back up and into the basket.

rebounding—This is grabbing the ball, shot by a teammate or opponent, that misses and bounces off the rim or backboard.

set shot—The player simply plants himself and, without jumping, shoots the ball.

shooting guard—Also called the Two Guard. This player, usually one of the team's primary scorers, is expected to hit most of his two-point shots and connect with the three-pointers. Michael Jordan, Jeff Hornacek, and Mitch Richmond are great shooting guards.

small forward—This player also is called the Three Man. These players can handle the ball well and are normally skilled scorers, hitting jumpers, going to the hoop through the defense for layups or dunks. They also are often fine defenders. Scottie Pippen and Dominique Wilkins are fine small forwards.

three-pointer—A shot that comes from beyond the three-point line, twenty-two feet or further from the basket.

tip-in—A player jumps and taps in a teammate's shot that has missed and is bouncing off the rim or backboard.

FURTHER READING

Aaseng, Nathan. *Sports Great David Robinson.* Springfield, N.J.: Enslow Publishers, Inc., 1992.

Benagh, Jim. *Basketball: Startling Stories Behind the Records.* New York: Sterling Publishing Company, 1991.

Biesel, David B. *Can You Name That Team?: A Guide to Professional Baseball, Football, Soccer, Hockey & Basketball Teams and Leagues.* Lanham, Md.: Scarecrow Press, 1991.

Bjarkman, Peter C. *The Encyclopedia of Pro Basketball Team Histories.* New York: Carroll & Graf Publishers, 1994.

Knapp, Ron. *Top 10 Basketball Centers.* Springfield, N.J.: Enslow Publishers, Inc., 1994.

Garber, Greg. *Hoops: Highlights, History, & Stars.* Michael Friedman Publishing Group, 1994.

Hill, Bob, and Randall Baron. *The Amazing Basketball Book: The First 100 Years.* Louisville, Ky.: Devyn Press, 1991.

One Hundred Greatest Basketball Players. New York: Random House Value Publishing, 1989.

Pluto, Terry. *Loose Balls: The Short Wild Life of the American Basketball Association—As Told by the Players, Coaches, & Movers & Shakers Who Made It Happen.* New York: Simon and Schuster Trade, 1991.

Sullivan, George. *All About Basketball.* New York: Putnam Publishing Group, 1991.

The San Antonio Spurs Basketball Team

INDEX

WHERE TO WRITE

San Antonio Spurs
Alamodome
100 Montana St.
San Antonio, TX 78203

WEBSITE
http://www.nba.com/spurs/

The San Antonio Spurs Basketball Team